Praise for *The Imagination Station® books*

The jaguar was so cool. I love this book; well, I love them all. I asked my daddy about baptism, and now I want to get baptized because I have already asked Jesus in my heart.

—Kinley, age 6, Colorado Springs, Colorado

I really enjoy traveling through time and going on adventures in the Imagination Station. I can't wait to see where they go in the next book!"

—Chance, age 8, Congerville, Illinois

As an MK who grew up in Ecuador (and attended the Nate Saint Memorial School), I have been deeply influenced by the story and people reflected in this book. *In Fear of the Spear* draws from a powerful, true story of forgiveness. The book combines adventure, intrigue, suspense, tragedy, and joy in a way that will capture and inspire the hearts of young readers.

—Mary L., mom and editor, Wheaton, Illinois

More Praise for The Imagination Station® books

Excellent series, inspiring and encouraging for young readers who are building their faith.

—Terri F., children's author and mom, Nineveh, Indiana

My normally reluctant reader devoured [*Voyage with the Vikings*] and nearly completed two books in one evening. I have never seen him this excited to read!

—Chandra H., happy mom, League City, Texas

Lessons on faith and history—all wrapped up in one exciting edge-of-your-seat adventure! Imagination Station scores another home run for young readers.

—Nancy S., children's author, Chino, California

The [Imagination Station] books are really awesome. I hope they write a thousand more! I'm totally gonna read these to my son when I'm a dad. I want to read these books a thousand, million infinity times!

—Hamish, age 6, Colorado Springs, Colorado

FOCUS ON THE FAMILY PRESENTS

In Fear of the Spear

BOOK 17

MARIANNE HERING
ILLUSTRATED BY DAVID HOHN

TYNDALE

FOCUS ON THE FAMILY • ADVENTURES IN ODYSSEY®
TYNDALE HOUSE PUBLISHERS, INC. • CAROL STREAM, ILLINOIS

In Fear of the Spear

© 2016 Focus on the Family

ISBN: 978-1-58997-804-1

A Focus on the Family book published by Tyndale House Publishers, Inc., Carol Stream, Illinois 60188.

Focus on the Family and Adventures in Odyssey, and the accompanying logos and designs, are federally registered trademarks, and The Imagination Station is a federally registered trademark of Focus on the Family, 8605 Explorer Drive, Colorado Springs, CO 80920.

TYNDALE and Tyndale's quill logo are registered trademarks of Tyndale House Publishers, Inc.

This is a work of fiction. The scenes in chapter 6 are loosely based on real events. The characters Kimo, Rachel Saint, and Steve Saint are historical people; however, all their dialogue and scenes are drawn from the author's imagination.

Cover design by Michael Heath | Magnus Creative

Library of Congress Cataloging-in-Publication Data for this title is available at http://www.loc.gov.

Printed in the United States of America
16 17 18 19 20 21 22
1 2 3 4 5 6 7 8 9 10 /

For manufacturing information regarding this product, please call 1-800-323-9400.

To LKW, BDE, and PEM for believing in me.

—MKH

Contents

Prologue

Doomsday in Pompeii began with Patrick
sitting alone in the Imagination Station.
Lightning struck Whit's End. The electricity
zapped the machine's computer. However,
the Imagination Station still took Patrick
on an adventure, but it gave him the wrong
gifts: a saddlebag, bandanas, and a sheriff's
badge.

But Beth and Eugene didn't know where
Patrick had gone. Beth found some of Whit's

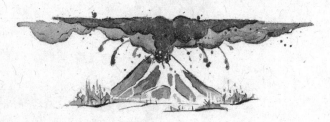

notes about volcanoes and Mount Vesuvius. Eugene figured out that the Imagination Station had sent Patrick to Pompeii.

Eugene and Beth realized that Patrick could be killed if the volcano erupted. They knew they had to save him. But how?

In the workshop, Beth uncovered an older version of the Imagination Station. It looked like a car. Eugene programmed it so that she could find Patrick.

Beth arrived in ancient Pompeii in time to save Patrick from the lava. Then *both* Imagination Stations appeared.

Beth ran to the helicopter-like machine that had been struck by lightning. She sat

down and then pushed the red button.

Patrick rushed to the car-like one.

● ● ●

From *Doomsday in Pompeii* . . .

The old Imagination Station felt like riding in a car. It had wild colors spinning on the windshield. Patrick felt as if the

machine slowed to a stop.

Mr. Whittaker's workshop slowly appeared in front of Patrick.

"What a ride!" he said as he climbed out.

Suddenly Eugene was at his side.

"Patrick!" he said. "Thank God you're safe!"

"That was close," Patrick said.

"Where's Beth?" Eugene asked.

"She's in the other Imagination Station," Patrick replied.

They raced to the other machine. It sat very still and dark.

"Oh no," Eugene said.

Patrick pushed the button to open the door. Nothing happened.

"What's wrong? Where's Beth?" Patrick asked.

Eugene groaned and said, "I don't know."

The Jaguar

Beth stepped out of the Imagination Station.

She knew one thing right away. She wasn't at Whit's End.

Thick, lush bushes surrounded her. She heard a bird whistle from somewhere above.

She looked in the direction of the sound. Tall trees seemed to stretch to heaven. They blocked most of the sunshine. Their thick trunks were covered in vines.

She moved a few yards into a small

clearing.

"Patrick!" she called. "Patrick! Are you here?"

She listened carefully for an answer. She strained her ears. But all she heard was a lovely mixture of bug, bird, and jungle sounds.

Water was flowing somewhere close by. Hoots and clicks and buzzing filled her ears. And monkeys chattered. Or was it something else?

She looked back at the Imagination Station. It was still there.

"That's strange," she whispered. "Usually it disappears right away."

Beth suddenly felt cold. The dark shadows of the trees felt spooky. The air was thick with moisture and lingered in her lungs. A large mosquito landed on her hand.

"Take that!" she said, slapping the insect away.

In response, she heard leaves rustling behind her. She turned.

Was that a face in the bushes? She blinked and looked again. The face was gone.

Grrr. A soft but menacing growl sent chills up her neck.

Beth turned and saw a jaguar.

Its fur was golden brown with black splotches. The huge cat perched in the V of a tree trunk. Its long tail flicked quickly.

Beth thought that it must have just jumped into the tree.

"Nice kitty kitty," Beth said, cooing. "I hope you've eaten a tasty snack or two today."

The cat growled again. Its golden eyes were the color of a glowing jack-o'-lantern.

Beth had only one hope for safety. But that meant turning her back on the big cat.

She took a deep breath. Then she pushed through the bushes. She lunged toward the Imagination Station. She stretched out an arm to touch the door.

But instantly the machine faded. Her hand felt nothing.

She gasped and stared into the vast jungle.

The Workshop

"To the computer!" Eugene cried. He moved quickly to the desk with the laptop. "I'll check the coordinates of the original Imagination Station."

Patrick followed and looked over Eugene's shoulder.

Eugene was working hard. He was punching keys and opening and closing websites.

Once in a while, lightning would strike. A

kaboom would shake the building. And then the lights would flicker. The storm reminded Patrick of how all the trouble started.

"Is she at the World Cup?" Patrick asked. "That's where I was supposed to be. But then the Imagination Station got zapped and it broke."

"I appreciate the suggestion," Eugene said. "But I took it upon myself to erase that trip before Beth left."

"How about the one before that?" Patrick asked.

Eugene shook his head. He said, "Indeed, I deleted *all* the adventures. I feared the lightning strike had corrupted them. Both of you should have come back here. It's the default for both Imagination Stations."

"Default?" Patrick asked.

Eugene stopped typing. He rubbed his

forehead. "It was the backup plan," he said softly. "Beth should be here. That's what I programmed."

Patrick put a hand on his shoulder. "You haven't lost her," Patrick said. "She's just gone somewhere else. Mr. Whittaker will know where she is."

"No doubt he would," Eugene said. "But he's not answering." He pushed a cell phone across the desk.

Patrick picked it up. He opened the phone screen. There were thirty-seven calls to Whit's cell phone in the last ten minutes.

"What about Connie?" Patrick asked. "She always knows where Mr. Whittaker is. Or at least it seems like it. Maybe she can tell us."

Eugene's voice trailed off. "Miss Kendall?"

"Sure," Patrick said. "Maybe Mr. Whittaker told her where he was going."

Patrick slid the phone back to Eugene.

"It's worth a try," Eugene said.

Beth turned around.

The jungle cat had leaped into the air. Its front legs were outstretched. She could see its white belly.

Beth's heart stopped. Her throat closed with panic. She couldn't even shout for help.

Suddenly a shot rang out.

Bam!

The cat twisted in midair. It let out a screech at the same time. *Ya-rarh!*

Then another shot. *Bam!*

The beast landed a few feet from Beth.

Then it sprang into the bushes.

Beth leaned against a tree. She took a few deep breaths, closing her eyes.

God, she prayed, *thanks for saving my life.*

Eugene called Connie Kendall using the computer and a microphone. He turned on the speakers.

R-r-ring. R-r-ring.

Connie answered on the third ring.

"Hey, Eugene," Connie said.

"Greetings, Miss Kendall," Eugene said. "We're in a rather desperate situation. Do you know the whereabouts of Mr. Whittaker?"

"This is about Whit?" Connie asked. "You want to know where he is?"

"Yes, please!" Eugene said.

"I have no idea," she said.

Patrick's hopes fell. He had been sure Connie would have answers.

Connie went on, "He was all secretive last time I saw him. I knew he was leaving the state, but that's it."

"So he didn't give you any contact information? A phone number, perhaps?" Eugene asked.

"He hasn't even sent a text,"

Connie said. "He's probably off somewhere fishing. He may have turned off his phone. He wouldn't want the phone to scare the bait or anything."

"You mean scare the fish," Eugene said. "Have a wonderful afternoon."

"Wait a minute!" Connie said. "What's the desperate situation you're in? Can I help?"

"It's too complicated to explain right now," Eugene said.

Patrick decided to cut in. He leaned closer to the microphone.

"Where did Mr. Whittaker go on his last trip in the Imagination Station?" he asked. His voice was a bit shaky.

"Hi Patrick," Connie said. "Your voice sounds funny. This is Patrick, right?"

Patrick cleared his throat. "Ummm . . . yeah," he said. "Hi."

"Whit went to measure the temperature of molten lava," Connie said.

Eugene took over. "Do you remember anything about his trips before the lava?"

"Not really," Connie said. "He said he was programming adventures just for him. He said they were too dangerous for me, at least while he was testing."

Eugene suddenly sat upright. "Too dangerous for you?" he said. Then he softly added, "Beth, what have we done to you?"

Patrick sucked in his breath.

Connie sighed. "All I know is that he bought a new laptop. That was a week ago," she said. "He said something about meeting a great saint. Oh, and something about a quarter."

"Which saint, Miss Kendall?" Eugene asked. "Could you possibly be precise?"

"Sorry," Connie said. "There are dozens of them, aren't there?"

Eugene sighed.

Patrick asked, "What was the quarter about?"

"Yikes," Connie said, "my roof is leaking! I've got to get a bucket. I'm sorry I don't know any more. Can I let you guys go?"

"Yes," Eugene said. "We'll attempt—"

Patrick heard a click. The call was over.

Dr. Silva

Beth saw a man step through the bushes a few seconds later.

He stared at Beth through large-rimmed glasses.

Beth stared back.

The man was wearing clothes that were sort of normal. They appeared to be American. But they were out of date.

She looked at her own outfit. Her clothes were like his: khaki pants and long-sleeved, white cotton shirts. Each of them wore a vest.

But there was one main difference. The man held a rifle.

"Thank you for saving me," Beth said. "I thought for sure the jaguar was going to attack me."

The man raised a finger to his lips. Beth knew he wanted her to be quiet.

She nodded and watched him silently.

He squatted and looked at the paw prints the large cat had made. Then he studied the leaves on the nearby bushes. He crawled a few feet into the bushes. Then he came back and brushed off his pants.

"Did the bullets hit the jaguar?" he whispered.

Beth leaned in close to him. "I don't know," she whispered. "It jerked in midair and screeched."

"There's only a little blood," he said quietly.

Beth felt relieved that the cat was only nicked. She had been afraid of the jaguar. But she didn't want it hurt.

"I'm Beth," she said in hushed tones.

He looked at Beth and gave a faint smile. "I'm Dr. Silva," he said.

Beth smiled back.

"Are you a hunter?" she whispered.

"Sort of," he said softly. "I'm a botanist. I hunt for rare plants. Who's Patrick? I heard you shouting his name."

"My cousin," Beth said.

"We need to find him and go," he whispered. "This place is dangerous. Your shouts and the rifle shots were loud. The noises must have alerted the Aucas."

"Aucas?" Beth asked.

Dr. Silva's eyes grew large as if in wonder.

"You must know about them," Dr. Silva said. "I think they're savages. They killed dozens of Shell Oil workers a few years ago."

Beth shook her head.

She heard a mosquito buzz her ear. A monkey swung through the trees above them. Colorful birds hopped from branch to branch.

She saw movement in the bushes. *Had the jaguar come back?* she wondered.

Dr. Silva said, "Hurry! Let's go!" He spread the bushes with his rifle. He rushed headlong into the jungle where the Imagination Station had been. Then suddenly he fell facedown.

His rifle slipped out of his hands. It landed several feet away from him.

Beth noticed an odd-looking white bag at Dr. Silva's feet. She decided he must have tripped. She heard a noise and looked up.

"Ummm, do Aucas carry long spears?" she asked. She wanted to make sure before she panicked.

Dr. Silva moaned. "Yes," he said. "They can throw them hard and on target." He pushed himself to his knees.

"And long blowguns?" she asked.

"Yes," Dr. Silva said. "They hunt small animals with poison darts. The blowguns shoot more than a hundred feet away." He was squatting now.

"I think you should look up," Beth said.

"Why?" Dr. Silva asked.

"Aucas," Beth whispered. "Complete with spears and blowguns. And they don't wear much clothes."

Dr. Silva stood. He looked up at the men surrounding them. He moaned again.

"Savages kill on sight," he said. "We're done for."

4

Aucas

Eugene was typing quickly into the computer. "Here's a list of great saints," he said. "We'll just have to find one who lived in a dangerous place."

"Didn't most of the saints live in boring old churches?" Patrick asked. He was standing behind Eugene. "I thought all they did was pray."

Eugene chuckled. "Joan of Arc helped the king of France win back his throne," he said.

Patrick looked at her picture. "She's wearing armor!" he said. "And I didn't know they made girl saints."

Eugene said, "I don't think Mr. Whittaker visited her recently. There's already an Imagination Station adventure that tells Joan's story. He wouldn't need a new one."

"I forgot about Saint Patrick of Ireland," Patrick said. "I met him on an adventure too. So cross him off the list." He thought a moment. "What about that guy with the birds on his shoulder? I saw a statue of him."

"Yes!" Eugene said. "Saint Francis. He fought in the Crusades."

"That's dangerous!" Patrick shouted.

Eugene began researching about Saint Francis. The keyboard clicked as he typed.

Patrick said, "But don't forget what

Connie said. Was there a quarter of a century or another word like it? Search for the words 'a quarter.'"

Eugene's fingers froze above the keyboard. "Say that again," he said. "Fast."

"A quarter," Patrick blurted.

"Faster," Eugene said.

"A quarter, a quarter, a quarter!" Patrick cried. "I get it now!"

Eugene stood up. Then he turned to face Patrick.

"Ecuador!" they said at the same time.

Dr. Silva crawled toward his rifle. Just as he moved, a young Auca warrior stepped out of the bushes.

"Watch out!" Beth shouted.

The Auca grabbed the rifle barrel. The weapon slid away from Dr. Silva's grasp.

"Oh, blast it!" Dr. Silva said.

Beth moved closer to Dr. Silva. She waited while he got to his feet.

The Auca men made no move toward them. They just stood there, staring. Their spears and blowguns weren't pointed at Beth or Dr. Silva.

"We're not dead yet," Beth said. "Why?"

"I don't know," Dr. Silva said. He brushed wet leaves off his pants. "Maybe they think we have help. Does your cousin carry a gun or a rifle?"

"Patrick is in elementary school," she said.

Dr. Silva laughed.

Beth didn't think it was a happy sound.

She leaned against his side. "Stay close to me," she whispered. "Maybe they won't kill children. Especially not a young girl."

The American man snorted. But he draped

his arm across Beth's shoulders anyway.

"Don't count on mercy from this lot," he said.

Eugene's Adventure

Patrick asked Eugene, "Is there a great saint from Ecuador?"

Eugene gasped. "There is someone. But not a saint in the way we were thinking," he said.

"Then why did Mr. Whittaker want to meet him?" Patrick said.

Eugene sat down. "It's a sad story," he said. "I don't have time to tell it. I need to program it."

He went to the car-like Imagination
Station.

"Oh," Patrick said, "Beth." He felt guilty.
For a few minutes he had been focused only
on finding the saint.

"Yes, Beth," Eugene said. "It's imperative
that I go and assist her." He opened the
trunk and fiddled with a panel hidden
inside. Then he slammed it shut.

"Uh-uh," Patrick said. He shook his head.
"You have to stay here. What if something
goes wrong again?"

"It's my responsibility and, therefore, my
adventure," Eugene said. "I say we both go.
And I'll bring this with me." He motioned to
the laptop and picked it up.

Patrick nodded. He sat down in one of the
car seats. "Are you sure?"

Eugene sat down on the other seat. "No,"

he said. "But it's the only way I can think of to help Beth. *And* keep track of you!"

Suddenly Eugene's mood brightened. "I know," he said. "I can put the Imagination Station in lockdown mode."

Eugene shut his door.

Patrick closed his door too.

They were snug inside the car.

"What does 'lockdown mode' mean?" Patrick asked.

"Mr. Whittaker programmed this first Imagination Station for the government," Eugene said. "The project was . . . canceled. But it had some interesting features. No one could interfere with top-secret or life-changing events. That's lockdown mode."

Eugene opened the glove box. He pulled out several pairs of gloves: knit ones, leather ones, and one pair of mittens that had red buttons sewn on for decoration. He reached inside again.

Patrick heard a soft thud as if a lever had been released.

Then Eugene put the gloves back inside and closed the box.

"Let's go," Patrick said. He turned the steering wheel. The windshield immediately began to spin. Swirls of color circled his eyes like a kaleidoscope.

A few seconds passed. Patrick heard a high-pitched whistle. Then Eugene shouted, "Stop the train! Stop the train!"

Now Patrick couldn't see or hear anything else. He jerked on the wheel, but nothing changed. He had a sinking feeling in the pit of his stomach. Something had gone very wrong.

The Yellow Plane

The Aucas had taken Beth and Dr. Silva to their village.

Their long houses were made of tree trunks and palm branches.

Beth and Dr. Silva waited inside one of the houses. An Auca warrior stood at each entrance.

"At least we have food," Beth said to Dr. Silva.

The guard had given her a plain wooden

bowl. It was filled with papaya slices.

She picked up a slice. She scooped away the black seeds and took a bite.

"They're just trying to keep us healthy," Dr. Silva said. "They will torture us later."

"I thought you said the Aucas killed on the spot," Beth said. Papaya juice dripped down her chin. She wiped it off with the back of her hand.

"They do," Dr. Silva said. "Something's not right." He paced from wall to wall.

Hammocks and an old trunk were the only things inside the house. Beth put the bowl on the trunk.

The teen Auca entered. He carried the white bag that Dr. Silva had tripped over. He plopped it down and then left the house.

Beth looked at the small bag the Imagination Station had left. The fabric and rope were handmade. She felt sure it contained the gifts for the Pompeii adventure. The Imagination Station was giving out the wrong gifts for the wrong adventures.

"That was nice of him," Beth said.

Dr. Silva picked up the bag. "It's a trick," he said.

He peered inside and then reached into the small bag. He pulled out a black mask. It looked like a Halloween mask for a bug costume.

"Oh," Beth said. "I think the mask is mine. I needed it . . . on vacation a few days ago."

"Oh?" Dr. Silva asked. His eyes narrowed. "Were you in a war zone? That's a military-grade gas mask. I've never seen one this advanced."

"Well," Beth said, "it's always nice to be

prepared." She flashed a bright smile.

Dr. Silva peeked into the little bag. "If the bag is yours, tell me what else is inside."

It was a challenge.

Beth hesitated. The botanist seemed to distrust her. What would Mr. Whittaker have sent her?

"A map . . ." she said, guessing.

Dr. Silva pulled out a piece of parchment. He whistled. "This looks ancient," he said. He unrolled the thick paper. "The writing is in Latin."

He looked at Beth. "What are you doing with a priceless historic map?" he asked.

Beth gulped. What could she tell him?

The Imagination Station became very still. The windshield was dark.

Patrick looked to his side. The seat next

to him was empty. Eugene was gone!

What's happening? Patrick wondered. *Has Eugene gone back to Whit's End? Why did he shout about a train?*

Suddenly the car's windshield cleared. Patrick could see out.

The machine had landed near a river. The water was clear. White sandbars bordered the water. Thick, tall trees stretched ahead as far as Patrick could see. Ecuador was beautiful.

He wanted to look for Beth and Eugene. He pulled on the door handle. It wouldn't move. He leaned his shoulder against the door. Nothing. He tried rolling down the window. It held fast.

Something outside captured his attention. He looked up.

A small, yellow plane flew above the

river. It landed on a sandbar very near the Imagination Station.

Several young men got out of the plane. Their hair was short. Most of them wore white T-shirts and plain tan pants.

One of them was wearing jeans. He saw Patrick and waved.

Patrick waved back.

"History of missions, Operation Auca," a voice from inside the car said. The tone sounded like a newsman's. "The setting is the rain forest of Ecuador."

Patrick looked at the ceiling of the car Imagination Station. Three small speakers were almost hidden in the lining.

"The year is 1956," the speakers blared. "The young missionary men are Peter Fleming, Roger Youderian, Ed McCully, Jim Elliot, and Nate Saint."

"He's the saint!" Patrick shouted. "This is it! This is where Mr. Whittaker went!"

The voice said, "On the shore of Palm Beach, the men meet several members of an Auca clan.

"The missionaries exchange gifts with the Aucas. They communicate with hand motions. The missionaries believe the clan will be peaceful. Operation Auca's goal is to present the gospel to this people group."

Patrick wanted out of the car. He tried pulling on the steering wheel. It wouldn't budge. He tried opening the glove box. It was shut tight.

"The five martyrs . . ." the speaker said.

"Martyrs!" Patrick screamed. "That means they died! No! I have to save them! This lockdown mode stinks."

He pounded on the windshield. The man

who waved to him wasn't looking. He was walking toward two women with long, black hair. They had come from the jungle. They looked as if they could be Aucas.

"No!" shouted Patrick once more.

"The five martyrs die on January 8," the speakers announced and then went silent. The windshield started to spin. Bright colors swirled.

Patrick was forced into his seat. This adventure was over.

Nemo

"Well," Dr. Silva said, "What about the map?"

Beth told the truth. "It belongs to a friend of mine," she said. "He likes studying active volcanoes. The mask was to protect against the poisonous gases."

"Volcano?" he said and shook his head. "You are very lost. The nearest active volcano in Ecuador is hundreds of miles west."

Dr. Silva shook out the white bag.

Six bone-shaped biscuits fell out. They

landed on the ground and broke into crumbs.

Dr. Silva looked puzzled. "There aren't any dogs around here either," he said.

Suddenly she heard the Auca men shouting. It sounded like, "*Menye! Menye!*"

Beth ran to the edge of the house and looked out. Several Aucas rushed into the jungle with spears.

But one of the guards stayed at the hut's entrance. He stood spear in hand, strong and silent.

The car-like Imagination Station stopped again.

Patrick watched, amazed, as the door opened by itself. He quickly left the car.

He was in a similar jungle. But he stood in a clearing, and there was no river.

Not far away was a large, white two-story house. A deck stretched along one side. It had concrete bricks underneath to keep it lifted off the ground.

Turning, Patrick saw an even larger barn-like building. It was near a long strip of cleared land. He wondered what it was for.

A mechanical buzzing noise came from above.

Patrick looked up, hoping to see the yellow plane. But this plane was white. And it was coming straight toward him.

The doctor came over and stood behind Beth.

"Now's our chance," he said.

"Chance for what?" Beth asked.

"Most of the Aucas have left," he said. "There's only one guard now. We can make a run for it."

Beth shook her head. "He'll track us," she said.

"That's a risk I'm willing to take," Dr. Silva said.

The Auca guard moved toward them. The botanist backed into the hut. He sat next to the trunk.

Beth stood her ground. She couldn't read the Auca's expression. *Is he worried? Is he angry?*

The guard started to draw in the sand with his spear. He looked at Beth and started to talk. His words had a lot of *o* and *b* and *k* sounds.

Beth smiled and nodded.

He smiled and nodded too. Then he began to draw again.

Beth couldn't tell what the picture was. *Is*

it a map? she wondered.

Beth turned and walked slowly into the hut.

"What was he trying to tell you?" Dr. Silva asked.

"Something very strange," Beth said. "I think he wants to find Nemo!"

The White Plane

Patrick ran toward the house, away from the cleared area.

The small, white plane approached the ground. It had three wheels. Two wheels were in the front. One was at the back.

The engine buzz was loud. Patrick covered his ears with both hands.

The plane's front wheels hit the dirt runway. There was a screeching sound. The plane's tail bounced and landed again. Then

the plane rolled a few hundred yards to a
stop.

The engine was off, but the propeller kept
spinning slowly.

Patrick now ran toward the plane. He
hoped Beth would be on board.

A little door on the side of the plane
opened. An older, blond boy in shorts
jumped out. His white canvas tennis shoes
hit the ground. He ran and came straight
toward Patrick.

Patrick slowed, waiting for the boy to join
him.

"I'm Steve!" the boy said. "Who are you?"

Beth looked at the dog biscuit pieces on the
ground. A mass of reddish ants swarmed
over the broken bits. A few of the ants
carried crumbs in their tiny jaws.

Beth shuddered, hoping the ants wouldn't sting her. She couldn't stand insects.

Dr. Silva didn't seem to be bothered by the ants. He motioned for Beth to join him at the back of the house.

"Our best chance at escape is now. I have to fight off only one Auca," he whispered. "I'm going to run out the back entrance. The guard will probably chase me. Then you run the other way. Hide in the jungle until it's safe."

"How will I find you?" Beth asked.

Dr. Silva was silent for a while. He seemed to be thinking.

"My camp is east of here," he said finally. "Not far from where we met. It's near a stream. Six fallen trees form a small bridge. Look for that."

"I don't think I can find it easily," Beth

said. "Everything in the jungle looks the same to me."

"I can draw you a map," he said. "There may be paper in here." Dr. Silva opened the little trunk.

They looked inside it.

"Blouses and skirts?" Beth said.

"This is what Ecuadorian women wear," Dr. Silva said.

Beth lifted out a pretty, light-blue shirt.

"Why do you think these are here?" Beth asked. "The Aucas don't wear these kind of clothes."

"Stolen," Dr. Silva said. He took out all the other clothes. A stack of books and papers were at the bottom of the trunk.

Beth smiled when she saw the top book. "It's a Bible," she said. "May I see it?"

Dr. Silva handed her the thin black Bible.

It had gold on the edges of the pages.

Beth opened the front cover. "It belongs to someone named Rachel," she said.

She looked at Dr. Silva. He was frowning.

"What's wrong?" she asked.

He held up some papers to answer her. They were pages from an old magazine. They had black-and-white photos on them.

Beth recognized one photo of an Auca man. He looked exactly like one of the men who had brought her to the hut.

Beth gasped. "Who are those women in the other photo?" Beth asked.

"The wives of five dead missionaries," Dr. Silva said.

"What happened to their husbands?" Beth asked.

"The men met with our Aucas," Dr. Silva said. "That was nine years ago, in 1956."

He dropped the papers back into the trunk. "I'm leaving *now*," he said. He slammed the trunk's lid. "Get safe. I'll find you by the bridge."

Beth watched Dr. Silva slip out the back of the hut. She shivered. She peered out of the grass house. She was alone with an Auca killer. And now he had Dr. Silva's rifle.

The Cockroach

The boy named Steve looked about thirteen. He wore jeans and a plaid shirt.

Patrick stuck out his right hand. "I'm Patrick," he said.

Steve grabbed Patrick's hand and shook it.

"Are you a missionary kid too?" Steve asked.

Patrick hesitated. He was a kid. And he was a missionary, because he knew it was important to share the Bible stories about Jesus.

"Yes," Patrick said at last. "I'm a missionary kid. And I need your help."

A woman got out of the plane. She came to join them.

She had a kind, round face and wore wire-rimmed glasses. Her light-brown hair had some gray hairs mixed in. It was pulled back and knotted at the back of her head.

Steve turned toward her. "Aunt Rachel," he said, "this is Patrick. He needs our help."

Rachel's eyebrows rose. She looked concerned.

"What's wrong?" Rachel asked. "How can Steve and I help?"

Patrick decided not to mention Eugene. He knew Eugene was on an adventure in a different time and place.

But he told them about Beth. He said she was lost in the jungle. He thought she might be near the Aucas' village.

"That's not good," Rachel said. "Many clans of the Aucas . . ." She paused. "They call themselves Waodani. Many Waodani clans are violent."

Patrick nodded. He remembered the martyrs he had seen on Palm Beach.

Steve asked, "What was Beth wearing?"

Patrick looked at his own tan pants and white shirt.

"Her clothes probably look like mine," Patrick said.

Rachel put a hand on each of the boys' backs. She moved them toward the white plane.

"Let's ask the pilot to refuel. Then we'll get back into the Courier," Rachel said. "The best way to find Beth quickly is by air. We've got to locate her by nightfall. Or else . . ."

"Or else what?" Patrick asked.

"Never mind," Steve said. "God will help us find her."

● ● ●

Beth's breathing quickened. She had to get out of that house and hide from the Aucas.

Zhuuurp.

Something large whizzed through the air. It brushed against Beth's hair before landing.

Beth cut off a scream by biting her bottom lip.

A cockroach was sitting on the little trunk. The bug was the size of a salad plate.

Beth got an idea. She picked up the empty white bag and opened

the top.

Beth quietly approached the cockroach. *Whoosh!* She covered it with the mouth of the bag.

The bug slid inside the cloth trap and wriggled.

"Gotcha!" Beth said.

Escape

Patrick sat right behind the pilot. Rachel sat in the copilot's seat. And Steve sat in a seat behind her.

Steve told Patrick that the plane was a Courier. The pilot helped Rachel by bringing mail, supplies, and medicine to the jungle. He was a missionary who lived in Quito, Ecuador. He spoke only Spanish.

The plane's engine buzzed as it sped down the runway. The Courier lifted off the ground. Patrick's stomach did a somersault.

He peered out the window. The jungle looked even more beautiful from above. Patrick thought the rain forest was like a giant salad. The trees seemed like large broccoli crowns and celery tops clumped together.

Wide green rivers curved through the jungle. They were shaped like giant question marks.

The plane flew very low. It must have frightened some parrots. They moved off as the plane approached. The flapping of their colorful wings was beautiful. It was the only motion Patrick could see.

His heart sank as the plane soared. Finding Beth would be almost impossible. It would be more difficult than finding a grain of salt in a sugar bowl.

Suddenly Steve shouted, "Waodani!"

Dr. Silva had been wrong. The Auca guard
didn't leave the house to chase him. Instead,
the Auca stood in front of the house. He
shouted into the jungle.

Beth thought he must be contacting the
other members of the clan. She knew she
had to leave the house quickly. Dr. Silva
might get too far ahead of her. She was
afraid she would never find him again.

The guard now faced away from her.
He was still looking into the jungle and
hollering.

Beth took the white bag, leaving the
ancient map behind. Then she sneaked out
the back of the house. She stared into the
thick trees and twisting vines.

Which way is east? she wondered. Since

she didn't know, she listened for the sound of water. She moved toward it.

Her heart beat louder with every second. Even her breaths sounded loud to her. She felt sure the Auca man would hear her. Surely he would capture her.

Beth tried to be quiet. But each step she took made a crunching sound. Certainly the man would be able to follow her tracks.

The cockroach in the bag wriggled and flapped its wings. It sounded way too noisy. Beth wished it would be still.

She noticed the rain forest had become much quieter. The Auca guard had stopped hollering.

He must know I'm gone, Beth thought.

The chase was on.

● ● ●

The plane banked and circled back.

Patrick could now see what Steve had noticed. A group of men with dark hair was on the move. They wore only loincloths. They carried spears and traveled quickly through the trees.

"Who are they?" Patrick asked.

"Those are our friends," Steve said.

"Friends?" Patrick asked.

"Yes," Steve said. "Aunt Rachel lives with a Waodani clan now. I get to stay with them during the summer."

"I thought you lived in the white house," Patrick said.

"I used to," Steve said. "But that was before . . ."

Patrick heard Rachel sigh.

"That was before the Waodani killed my brother," she said. "He was Steve's father."

Patrick gulped. He looked at Steve. "Is

your last name Saint?" he asked.

Steve nodded. "My dad's name was Nate. He died nine years ago," he said.

Rachel added, "Steve was only five years old when it happened."

"Are *all* the Waodani your friends now?" he asked.

"Goodness, no," Rachel said. "Most of the clans are still violent. Though we hope one day they'll accept the teachings of Jesus. That way they'll learn to forgive and stop killing one another."

Just then the pilot said "jaguar" with lots of *r* sounds at the end. He tapped the side window.

Patrick looked out the window again. He saw a yellow-and-black animal move through the trees.

Steve said, "The Waodani men must be

hunting the jaguar."

Killer Waodani and jaguars are down there, he thought. *What other dangers might hurt Beth?*

The Hollow Tree

Beth had to hide. But where?

She needed to rest, too. She ducked behind a wide, old tree. Its long, thick roots were exposed.

Beth leaned her shoulder against the tree. The bark cracked. She stepped away and kicked the bottom of the tree trunk.

The bark broke clear away.

"It's old and hollow," Beth whispered.

She kicked more of the bark away. Soon

she had made a nice hole at the bottom of the trunk.

She climbed inside and wedged her body up inside the trunk. She was careful not to crush the cockroach in the bag.

Inside was dark. It smelled sweet and damp at the same time. She listened intently to the jungle sounds.

A monkey howled. Birds squawked and chattered. And . . . an Auca man hollered.

He was close by.

Beth held her breath. She didn't want to make even a tiny sound.

Beth's legs began to itch. Then her rib cage and arms tingled. She brushed her right hand along her left arm.

She felt a trail of insects and then brushed them off.

Termites! she thought. *Gross!*

Beth slammed her knee into the tree trunk to get out. The bark split with a loud crack.

She kicked at the rest of the bark with all her might. The hole was now very large. She burst out of the tree into the light.

The first thing she saw was the Auca guard with the rifle.

Beth froze, but he didn't.

Using his hands, the man made a whistling sound. Then he started talking. Beth understood only one word: Nemo. He whistled again.

The sound made Beth's ears ache. But the noise also roused her.

He reached an arm out as if to grab her shoulder.

She quickly stepped back. She took the bag and loosened the ropes. Suddenly she tossed the bag at him.

The Auca's reflexes kicked in. He dropped the rifle and grabbed the bag.

The huge cockroach wriggled out and flew toward the Auca's face.

Beth had a few seconds to flee. She hurled herself headlong into the bushes.

Crocodile

Rachel asked the pilot to fly over the Waodani village.

"Our Waodani friends are chasing the jaguar," Rachel said loudly. "But your cousin wouldn't be with the hunters. If they had found her, they would have brought her to the village for safety."

The airplane buzzed along for a few minutes.

Patrick kept his eyes busy scanning the

vast green acres below.

He saw a small clearing in the distance. The pilot circled above it. The rectangular roofs of several grass houses came into view.

"No one is there," Steve said.

"That's odd," Rachel said.

"What would make everyone leave?" Patrick asked.

Rachel was silent. Patrick took his eyes away from the window.

He looked at the kind woman. She was frowning.

He looked at Steve. The young teen looked concerned.

"They might be out hunting," Rachel said. "Or they could be hiding from enemies."

"Who are their enemies?" Patrick asked.

"Another Waodani clan," Rachel said. "Sometimes they attack for revenge."

● ● ●

Beth found the stream at last. It was deeper than she imagined it would be.

Would Dr. Silva's camp be upstream or downstream?

She looked at the sun. Its position showed her which way to go. She went downstream.

Beth followed the stream by staying on the sandy edges. Roots and dead branches clumped near the water. She had to climb over them.

She heard a noise behind her. Beth whipped around.

Some leaves were rustling in the bushes. Had there been a face watching her? Or was

her imagination working overtime?

She ignored the feeling of being watched and moved on.

Beth finally found the bridge with six logs. She let out a small whoop for joy.

Dr. Silva was standing on the other side of the stream. He had a large bag slung over one shoulder.

"We need to run," Beth said. "The Auca man isn't far behind. And he has the rifle."

"I know," he said. He motioned with his head.

Beth turned around.

The man stepped out of the bushes. He had been close to Beth the whole time. It was as if he knew the jungle so well that he was part of it.

But Beth wasn't afraid to see him this time. She knew that he wasn't going to harm her.

The Auca had an odd expression on his face. But it wasn't anger.

Beth felt sorry that she had thrown the cockroach at him.

"We were foolish to think we could hide," Dr. Silva said.

Beth stood right at the edge of the stream. She put one foot on the bridge.

The Auca guard did nothing to stop her.

She took another two steps. She was a third of the way across.

Dr. Silva was moving an arm like a windmill. "Hurry," he said.

She took one more step, and suddenly the bridge moved. Beth lurched to the side. She waved her arms wildly to keep from falling.

The head of an animal appeared on top of

the logs. It looked like a crocodile. The skin
was bumpy, spotted, and gray. It's body was
as long as a man is tall. Its eyes looked as
if they were going to pop out of its head. Its
mouth was wide open.

Gaba

The plane banked and turned.

Patrick's stomach turned with it. He looked out the window to keep from getting dizzier.

"Where are we going?" Patrick asked.

The pilot said something in Spanish. Rachel said, "The pilot saw movement to the east."

Steve shouted a few seconds later. "I see a man!"

"Where?" Patrick asked.

Steve told Patrick exactly where to look.

The plane banked and flew lower.

Patrick saw the Waodani man. He was moving slowly along a winding path.

Patrick gasped. "He's been hurt," he said. "There's a spear in his side."

The plane circled again.

"We've got to help him," Patrick said.

"It will be difficult," Rachel said. "But we can land at Palm Beach. It's the closest landing strip."

Patrick gulped. Palm Beach was where the five martyrs had died nine years before.

Steve said, "I think it's Gaba."

"Yes, I can tell by his haircut," Rachel said "At least that's a small mercy."

Patrick was confused. "Small mercy?" he asked. A man had been wounded—how could that be a mercy?

Rachel reached her arm over the back of her seat. She offered her hand.

Patrick took it and felt Rachel's reassuring squeeze.

"It sounds terrible," she said, "but Gaba knows about God. In fact, he went to another clan to tell them about Jesus. Better that he is wounded than someone else."

Patrick still didn't understand. "Better than what?"

Steve said, "If Gaba dies, he'll go to heaven. That's better than someone dying who doesn't know Jesus. That's what my dad told me before . . . he died."

Patrick was silent. Steve's dad must have been a brave man. So was Gaba.

Rachel squeezed Patrick's hand once

more. Then she let it go.

Patrick looked out the window again.

Steve said, "I think I see your cousin!"

Beth screamed. She couldn't keep her balance on the log. She twisted her body away from the crocodile's open jaws.

Rows of yellowish teeth sat in the crocodile's pink gums. Some of the teeth were longer than others, like a dog's.

Beth fell into the stream. The water soaked her pants to the thighs.

Dr. Silva quickly reached toward Beth. He grabbed her upper arm. Then he hauled her out of the water.

Beth turned to watch the crocodile.

The Auca guard tried to fire the rifle. But there wasn't time. Instead, he held the rifle barrel. He slammed the thick end of the rifle down like a club.

Wham! The rifle handle hit the log.

The Auca raised the rifle again.

The crocodile shot forward, mouth open.

The guard jumped backward onto the land. The rifle slipped from his hands. It landed on the path.

The croc lunged at the man again.

"Watch out!" Beth shouted.

This time the Auca jumped to avoid the beast.

The reptile's gray spotted tail whipped back and forth.

The Auca wrapped one arm around the huge beast. The crocodile rolled into the water. The Auca man went with him.

"We've got to help him," Beth said. She tried to wrench her arm out of his grasp.

"No," Dr. Silva said. "There's nothing we

can do. This is our chance to escape."

Dr. Silva pushed her away from the bridge.

Beth turned her head to watch over her shoulder.

The man and the crocodile were thrashing in the stream. Water shot up in the air. That made it difficult for Beth to see. She couldn't tell if man or beast was winning the fight.

Beth looked at Dr. Silva. He was eyeing the rifle. It lay on the path across the bridge.

To get to the weapon, Dr. Silva would have to cross the bridge. He would have to pass the crocodile and the Auca.

Dr. Silva sighed. Then he pulled Beth harder away from the bridge.

Beth and the botanist slipped into the trees. They moved quickly and came to a clearing.

"Oh no," Beth said.

Dr. Silva dropped his bag. "What next?" he asked.

An Auca man was lying in the open grass. He had a spear in his side.

Reunions

Beth heard the buzz of an engine. She looked up. A small, white plane was banking toward the clearing.

Dr. Silva knelt beside the hurt Auca. "I think I can save him," Dr. Silva said. "If he lives, maybe the Aucas won't kill us."

Dr. Silva opened his bag. "I have some healing plants in here," he said. "They may help with the pain."

"Beth!" a voice called from the sky.

She looked toward the voice. The plane was close now. Someone was hanging out the window.

Patrick!

Beth's face broke into a grin.

"We're coming to help!" Patrick cried. "The man's name is Gaba!"

Beth waved. "Please hurry!" she shouted.

Patrick waved back.

The plane flew away.

Beth turned her attention to Gaba. She glanced at his wound. The opening was red and looked painful. She turned her head away.

"Is there anything I can do to help?" she asked Dr. Silva.

"I don't think so," Dr. Silva said. "He's tough, but he may go into shock."

Beth knew one thing that would help. She

hurried back toward the bridge.

The pilot landed the little plane smoothly.
Patrick recognized the landing area. It was
Palm Beach.

Rachel asked the pilot to radio for help.
She also asked him to stay with the plane.

The pilot nodded and picked up the radio.
He began speaking rapidly in Spanish.

Steve jumped out of the plane.

Rachel grabbed a white toolbox with a red
cross painted on it. It looked like a first aid
kit. She also jumped out of the Courier.

"This way," she said and then set off into
the jungle.

Patrick followed them.

Patrick was amazed that Rachel could
move so quickly through the rain forest.

He had to pay careful attention to his feet.

He watched where he put every step. He saw beetles, bugs, and unusual plants on the ground.

Suddenly Steve stopped. He held out an arm as if in warning.

Rachel paused. She whispered, "I see it."

"See what?" Patrick said. "Why did we stop?"

Grrr.

Patrick swiveled toward the growl. In a faraway tree sat a giant spotted animal.

The jaguar!

Beth stood face-to-face with the Auca guard. The rifle was back in his left hand. He was dripping wet, and his hair was messy. Those were the only signs he had just wrestled a crocodile.

"Gaba," Beth said.

The man looked curious. "Gaba?" he asked.

"Hurt," Beth said.

The man shook his head. Beth could tell he didn't understand.

Beth got an idea. She motioned as if being stabbed in the stomach. Then she lay on the ground, moaning.

The man's expression changed. He had understood!

Beth jumped up. She led the man back to the clearing.

When she got there, Dr. Silva was still kneeling next to Gaba.

The guard stood over his hurt friend. He held up his arms, palms up.

Beth thought he was praying.

Patrick saw something else move in the

bushes. A face maybe. But then the jaguar growled again and moved deeper into the jungle.

Steve, Rachel, and Patrick kept moving.

They came to the clearing. Patrick ran toward Beth.

"I'm so glad to see you," Patrick said. He hugged her quickly.

Beth whispered, "Let's stick together, no matter what."

Patrick nodded.

He looked around the clearing. A Waodani man was helping Gaba.

Rachel, Steve, and an American man with glasses were talking. The man looked like a Boy Scout leader.

"Who's he?" Patrick asked, motioning with his head.

"Who's she?" Beth asked in return. "And

the boy in jeans?"

Patrick shared his story about Palm Beach to Beth. He told her about the white house and meeting Steve and Rachel. He did not mention the part about Eugene disappearing.

Next, Beth explained about meeting Dr. Silva. She told him about the village and the magazine article. And she mentioned how afraid she had been.

When Beth used the word *Auca*, Patrick frowned. He told her that it wasn't a polite word. He said *Waodani* was what they wanted to be called.

"Come on," Patrick said. "I'll introduce you to Rachel and Steve."

The Showdown

Beth and Patrick moved toward the others. Dr. Silva, the guard, Rachel, and Steve were kneeling next to Gaba.

The wounded man was lying down again. His eyes were closed. The spear had been pulled out of his side. It lay next to him on the grass.

Dr. Silva was using gauze from a first-aid toolbox to clean Gaba's wound.

"Excuse me, Miss Rachel," Beth said.

Rachel looked up. Then she stood. "Why you must be Beth," the missionary said, smiling. "I'm so glad that you're safe."

"I am too, ma'am," Beth said. "Thank you for helping Patrick find me."

Rachel smiled again. "Steve helped," she said.

Beth said, "Thank you, Steve."

Steve said, "It turned out for the best. While we were looking for you, we saw Gaba. He needed our help too."

Beth asked, "What's the name of the Waodani man helping Gaba?"

Rachel said. "His name is Kimo."

The guard looked up at the sound of his name.

Beth grinned at Kimo and waved. She touched her breastbone and said, "Beth."

Kimo pointed at Rachel. "Nemo," he said.

Beth's eyebrow arched. "Nemo?" she echoed. "Kimo kept talking about you. But I couldn't understand him."

Rachel chuckled. "Nemo is my name in the Waodani language," she said. "It means star."

"Kimo took us to the village so we wouldn't get hurt," Beth said. "He wasn't trying to capture us."

"That's right," Rachel said. "There are other clans of Waodani. They might have speared you or Dr. Silva."

Beth thought, *Like they speared Gaba.*

Gaba moaned.

Rachel turned her attention away from Beth. "Is he going to live?" she asked Dr. Silva.

Dr. Silva put more green leaves over Gaba's wound. "I don't know," he said. "The bleeding won't stop. We've got to get him to a doctor."

Kimo said something to Rachel.

She looked at the blond teen. "Steve," she said, "please go find some clay and scrapings from a termite nest."

"Why?" Steve asked.

"Kimo says the Waodani mix those two things together. They use the paste to stop bleeding," Rachel said.

"I'm right on it," Steve said, standing.

Dr. Silva said, "I want to learn about this clay mixture. Please take some of my specimen jars and fill them." He stood and picked up his bag.

Pffft.

Beth heard the sound of something move quickly through the air. She turned toward the sound.

A long spear had pierced Dr. Silva's bag. Beth gasped.

"Someone tried to kill me!" Dr. Silva said. He held up the speared bag as proof.

"Not only you," Rachel said. "They may want to finish off Gaba!" The missionary moved closer to the hurt man. She used her body as if to shield him from harm.

Beth and Patrick rushed to help her. So did Dr. Silva and Kimo. As a group, they carefully carried Gaba away from the clearing. They lay his body behind the shelter of a large rock.

Beth peered out from behind the rock to look at Steve.

Steve was hidden by a thick tree. He seemed to be searching the jungle looking for the enemy. He shouted, "A warrior!"

The teen motioned to a spot across the

clearing.

A Waodani man had pushed through the trees. He had red stripes painted on his face.

Beth didn't remember him from the village. The war paint on his face made him look dangerous. She was glad his spear had missed Gaba.

Who is he? Beth wondered. *What does he want?*

The man with the war paint grunted when he saw Steve.

Kimo left Gaba and moved to the open area.

The new man laughed wickedly when Kimo came into view.

Patrick moved close to Beth. He whispered to her, "I saw that man's face in the bushes earlier."

"I think I did too," Beth said.

Rachel didn't take her eyes off Gaba. She was pressing gauze into his side. She said, "I recognize that man's laugh. That's Mipo. He lives in a hostile clan."

"Did he spear Gaba?" Beth asked.

"Yes," Rachel said. "Mipo thinks he gains more power when he kills."

Kimo shouted at Mipo. He rushed toward him, still shouting.

At first the two Waodani men circled each other like dogs about to fight. They were careful to stay out of each other's reach. Then Kimo made a move toward Mipo.

Mipo sidestepped him, shoving Kimo onto the grass.

Kimo rolled, and then sprang to his feet.

Mipo sprinted and lunged toward Dr. Silva's bag. He yanked out the spear. Laughing again, he balanced the spear in his hand. He turned and pointed the tip toward Kimo.

Kimo let out a loud yell.

Suddenly the jaguar ran through the clearing. It leaped gracefully into a tree.

Beth jumped up and moved toward the clearing on instinct. Patrick followed.

"Don't let them hurt it," she said to her cousin.

Ya-raow! the jaguar roared.

Everyone in the clearing was still now. They were watching the great cat.

The jaguar thrashed its tail. It seemed unafraid, waiting to attack.

Patrick was amazed at how large the jaguar was. Its muscles rippled under the thick fur. Its deep growls masked the other noises of the jungle.

Mipo, too, was now focused only on the big cat. His spear was ready and aimed at the animal.

Steve moved carefully between Patrick and Beth. The teen whispered, "The Waodani people believe whoever kills a jaguar will have great power."

The jaguar growled. It leaped to a low branch.

Kimo approached Mipo quietly, coming behind him. But he made no move to harm the warrior in war paint.

The botanist suddenly burst into the clearing. He held the rifle. "Mipo has to be stopped," Dr. Silva shouted. "He speared Gaba."

Steve shouted, "This isn't your business, Dr. Silva," he said. "The Waodani want to make peace with Mipo."

"That's impossible," Dr. Silva said. "Mipo is a savage. He can't change."

Dr. Silva fiddled with the rifle. There was a clicking noise. He aimed the rifle at Mipo's back.

Beth shouted, "Stop, Dr. Silva. Don't be a savage!"

Dr. Silva paused then he put a finger on the trigger.

Just then Kimo leaped across the clearing. He threw his shoulder into Dr. Silva's side. Kimo pushed hard on Dr. Silva's arm.

Bam! The rifle fired into the air.

Mipo turned his head for an instant.

The jaguar jumped from the branch straight toward Mipo. A terrible cry escaped from deep within its throat.

Ya-rarh!

Mipo hurled his spear in a wild arc at the

spotted cat.

Beth closed her eyes. She grabbed Patrick's arm for comfort. "No!" she cried.

The pointed spear peaked in the air and dropped. It missed the jaguar only by inches.

The big cat landed and hissed. It raised a huge paw and swiped at Mipo's chest.

Mipo gasped and staggered backward.

The jaguar gave one last growl. Then it disappeared into the lush jungle.

Mipo moaned softly. He leaned against a tree trunk.

Patrick saw three stripes of blood seep from Mipo's skin.

Kimo moved to where Mipo's spear had fallen. He picked it up. Then he lifted his knee and broke the spear in half.

Kimo took the rifle from Dr. Silva.

The botanist didn't resist.

Kimo emptied the rifle of the last bullets.

Dr. Silva picked up his bag. The hole made by the spear was the size of a grapefruit. He was careful not to let anything spill out.

"Let's get Gaba to a medical doctor before we're all killed," Dr. Silva said.

Patrick looked back at Mipo. But the warrior was gone.

Palm Beach

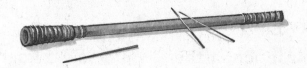

Kimo placed his hands underneath Gaba's shoulders. Dr. Silva's hands supported each of Gaba's ankles.

Steve and Patrick were on either side of the wounded man. Their hands were underneath his rib cage.

Rachel was standing nearby. She had Dr. Silva's bag over one arm. "On the count of three, lift," she said. "One, two, three!"

Beth was carrying the first aid kit. She

watched the men and boys gently raise Gaba's body.

Beth and Rachel led the way through the jungle. Sometimes Beth had to push back branches. At times she moved rocks off the narrow jungle paths.

"How much farther?" Beth asked Rachel.

"Not far," Rachel said. "Less than a mile. At this rate, maybe half an hour."

Beth kept a lookout for the jaguar. She was a little afraid it would come back. But she was more concerned about Mipo.

Sometimes she thought she saw faces hiding in the bushes.

"Do you think Mipo will attack us?" she asked.

Rachel said, "Perhaps. And bring others from his clan."

Dr. Silva spoke from behind them. "The laws of the jungle rule here. It's kill or be killed. Why do you live with these savages?"

Rachel said, "Because we're all savages, Dr. Silva. I needed Jesus to change my heart. Otherwise, I would be no different from Mipo."

"You would spear your enemies?" Dr. Silva asked.

Rachel chuckled. "Perhaps not spear them," she said. "But I would be selfish and filled with anger without Jesus. And I would be afraid of death."

"What changed Kimo?" Dr. Silva asked. "He and his clan could have killed me and Beth. But they didn't."

Rachel said that the Waodani clan were

afraid of the foreign men. And so they killed them with spears. Kimo had helped kill Nate Saint and the other four missionaries on Palm Beach.

Rachel explained that she and other relatives of the martyrs came to help. The women showed the Waodani people forgiveness. The Waodani didn't even have a word for forgiveness before that.

Rachel said that Kimo was the first Waodani to know Jesus.

"Kimo wanted to 'follow God's trail,'" Rachel said. "Over time, most of his clan decided to live by love. They no longer spear their enemies."

"So Jesus is why Kimo let Mipo live," Dr. Silva said. He had a look of wonder on his face.

There was a long silence after that. Beth

was thinking about what Dr. Silva had said. She prayed that Mipo would change one day.

Beth had been wondering about something. "I saw your trunk at the village," Beth said. "There was a magazine article inside. It was about the killings, wasn't it?"

"Yes," Rachel said. "The whole world knows about the deaths of the five martyrs. What the world needs to hear is that their deaths made a difference to the Waodani clan."

● ● ●

Kimo suddenly shouted. The group stopped moving forward.

Can Kimo hear things I can't? Patrick wondered. *Is Mipo coming back?*

Patrick's heart raced. No one in the group had a weapon. Kimo had broken Mipo's. spear. The rifle had been taken apart. It was in Dr. Silva's bag.

The bushes moved. Patrick saw a face. Then another.

Five Waodani men stepped onto the trail. Each man had a spear. One also had a machete.

Patrick wanted to drop Gaba and run. But he didn't. He closed his eyes and prayed instead.

Patrick opened his eyes and saw Rachel talking to the newcomers. *The men are friends.* He took a deep breath in relief.

The men quickly moved toward Gaba. They motioned that they wanted to help.

Patrick and Steve moved aside.

The Waodani men took over the job of carrying Gaba.

Beth watched as the group hurried through

the jungle.

"That was an answer to prayer," Rachel said. "Gaba needs to get to a medical doctor quickly."

Beth fell in step next to Patrick and Steve.

Steve asked Beth if he could carry the first aid kit.

Beth wasn't tired, but she let him take the white toolbox. "Thanks," she said.

They turned a corner. The river was just ahead.

The beach was beautiful. The day was almost over, but it was still sunny. The light glistened on the water and plant leaves.

There was a sputtering sound coming from above. Beth looked up. The little white plane was already in the sky taking Gaba to a doctor.

Everyone on the shore gathered. Rachel

said a prayer asking God to heal Gaba.

After she finished, Dr. Silva said, "I have a request."

"Oh?" Rachel said. "Do you want help looking for more plants?"

"That wasn't what I was thinking," Dr. Silva said. "I'd like to be baptized here."

Rachel smiled. "That can be arranged," she said. "Baptism means that you want to show others you are committed to Jesus. It shows you want to have your life changed."

"That's right," Dr. Silva said. "I want to walk His trail."

The baptism took only a few minutes. Kimo and Dr. Silva waded into the river.

Kimo said some words in the Waodani language.

Beth could tell it was a beautiful prayer.

Kimo's and Dr. Silva's faces looked

peaceful and joyful.

Then Kimo and Dr. Silva's arms intertwined. Kimo dipped Dr. Silva in the river.

The Train Whistle

Patrick heard the hum of the Imagination Station behind some bushes.

He nudged Beth gently.

"Look behind you," he whispered. He hooked a thumb over his shoulder.

Beth turned around. "There are both machines!" Beth said quietly.

"We need to go," Patrick said.

Beth nodded and said, "We've got to say good-bye first."

Beth hugged Rachel. She shook Steve's hand.

"Thanks for all you've done," Beth said. "Dr. Silva and Kimo are still in the river. Please tell them good-bye for us."

Patrick said, "I wish I could stay with you and the Waodani people. Learning to live in the jungle would be cool."

Steve said, "Maybe another time. I'll show you how to spear a fish."

"Will you be safe?" Rachel asked Patrick and Beth. "You can wait for the plane to come back."

Patrick looked over his shoulder at the Imagination Stations. "We know how to get home from here," he said.

At least I hope we do, he thought.

The cousins slipped into the jungle. They stood in front of the Imagination Stations.

Patrick couldn't decide which one to pick.

"Let's go in the helicopter one," Beth said.

"No," Patrick said. "It's still damaged from the lightning strike."

"Well," Beth said, "why not the car one?"

"That one's worse. Eugene got in it with me, but he disappeared," Patrick said.

"The Imagination Station sent you on different adventures!" Beth said. "It's never happened before."

"I don't know where or when Eugene went," Patrick said.

"There must be a clue," Beth said. She got in the car. She looked all over the seats and the dashboard. She tried to open the glove box. It was locked.

"I can't find anything useful," Beth said. "Think, Patrick. What happened?"

Patrick closed his eyes to help him

remember. "Right before Eugene disappeared, he said something weird," Patrick said.

"Tell me," Beth said.

Patrick looked worried. "I heard Eugene say, 'Stop the train!' He sounded scared."

"I would be scared too," Beth said quietly. "We have two choices. Neither one is perfect."

She held up her index finger. "Option one," she said, "we get into a broken machine."

Patrick looked at the helicopter Imagination Station. It had taken him to Pompeii by mistake. It was giving out the wrong gifts. And it had taken Beth here instead of back to Whit's End.

Beth held up a second finger. "Option two, we get into an Imagination Station that lands on a moving train."

"Or worse, on the train track," Patrick said.

Patrick looked at the car machine. It had been working fine until this last adventure. But Mr. Whittaker had programmed it for the government to use. Maybe it had hidden features which were causing problems.

"Maybe we should just stay here," Patrick said. "Mr. Whittaker will come find us."

"When?" Beth asked. "No one knows the day he's coming back."

Patrick sighed. "Let's take the car one," he said. "It has a lockdown mode. If it's too dangerous, it won't let us out."

"And maybe it will take us to Eugene," she said.

Patrick shrugged. "If it doesn't separate us too," he said.

The cousins sat in the comfortable black seats. They shut the doors.

Patrick gave the steering wheel a big spin.

Colors flashed on the windshield. They whirled like a kaleidoscope.

Patrick heard the shriek of a train whistle.

And suddenly everything went black.

Want to find out when book 18 will be released? Visit TheImaginationStation.com for more information.

Secret Word Puzzle

First Peter 3:21 is a verse about baptism.
Here is part of the passage:

"[Baptism] promises God that you will keep a
clear sense of what is . . .

—— —— —— —— —— —— ——

—— —— —— —— ——."

To complete this verse, start at the center
of the maze. Follow the paths until you find a
way out. Then highlight the letters along the
correct path. Write those letters on the lines
above. *But skip all the X letters.* The first word
you fill in is the Secret Word.

Secret Word Puzzle

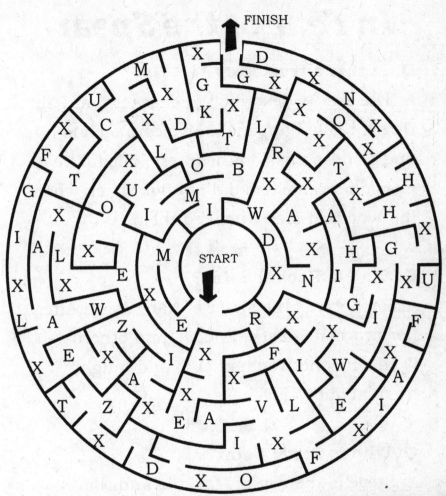

FINISH

START

Go to *TheImaginationStation.com.*
Find the cover of this book.
Click on "Secret Word."
Type in the answer,
and you'll receive a prize.

Questions about
In Fear of the Spear

Q: Is this a true story?

A: The events described in chapter 6 at Palm Beach really happened. Five courageous and selfless missionaries were killed. The missionary martyrs did not fight back when the Waodani men attacked them.

● ● ●

Q: Who is Rachel Saint?

A: Rachel was the sister of Nate Saint. After her brother's death, Rachel (and others) lived with the Waodani clan and taught them about forgiveness.

● ● ●

Q: Who is Steve Saint?

A: Steve is the son of Marjorie and Nate Saint, a missionary pilot. In 1965 Steve traveled to visit his Aunt Rachel for the summer. Kimo baptized Steve and his sister, Kathy, at Palm Beach. Steve and his family lived with the Waodani for a year after Rachel Saint died in 1994.

● ● ●

Q: My mom says there's a movie about the Waodani. Is that true?

A: There are *two* movies. In 2004 Steve Saint released a documentary called *Beyond the Gates of Splendor*. In 2006, a feature film called *The End of the Spear* came to theaters. When you're about thirteen years old, ask your parents if you can watch the films.

● ● ●

Q: Are Kimo, Gaba, and Mipo real people?

A: Kimo did become a Christian, but he didn't wrestle a caiman (an Ecuadorian croc). Gaba is a make-believe person modeled after a brave Waodani missionary named Tona. Mipo is not real at all, though the Waodani do wear red paint on their faces and hunt jaguars.

FOCUS ON THE FAMILY PRESENTS THE IMAGINATION STATION

THE KEY TO ADVENTURE LIES WITHIN YOUR IMAGINATION.

INDIGENOUS PEOPLE'S TECHNOLOGY AND EDUCATION CENTER

Want to learn about helping people like Kimo?

Visit ItecUSA.org (with a parent's help).
Here's the cool information you'll find:

- ways *you* can help spread the gospel worldwide
- why teaching the Waodani how to fill a cavity is *better* than sending a dentist
- video clips of the Waodani people
- facts about a *real* car that can fly
- news about Steve Saint

Want to build your own yellow Piper paper airplane?

You can do that too!
Go to itecusa.org/documents/n5156hmodel.pdf.